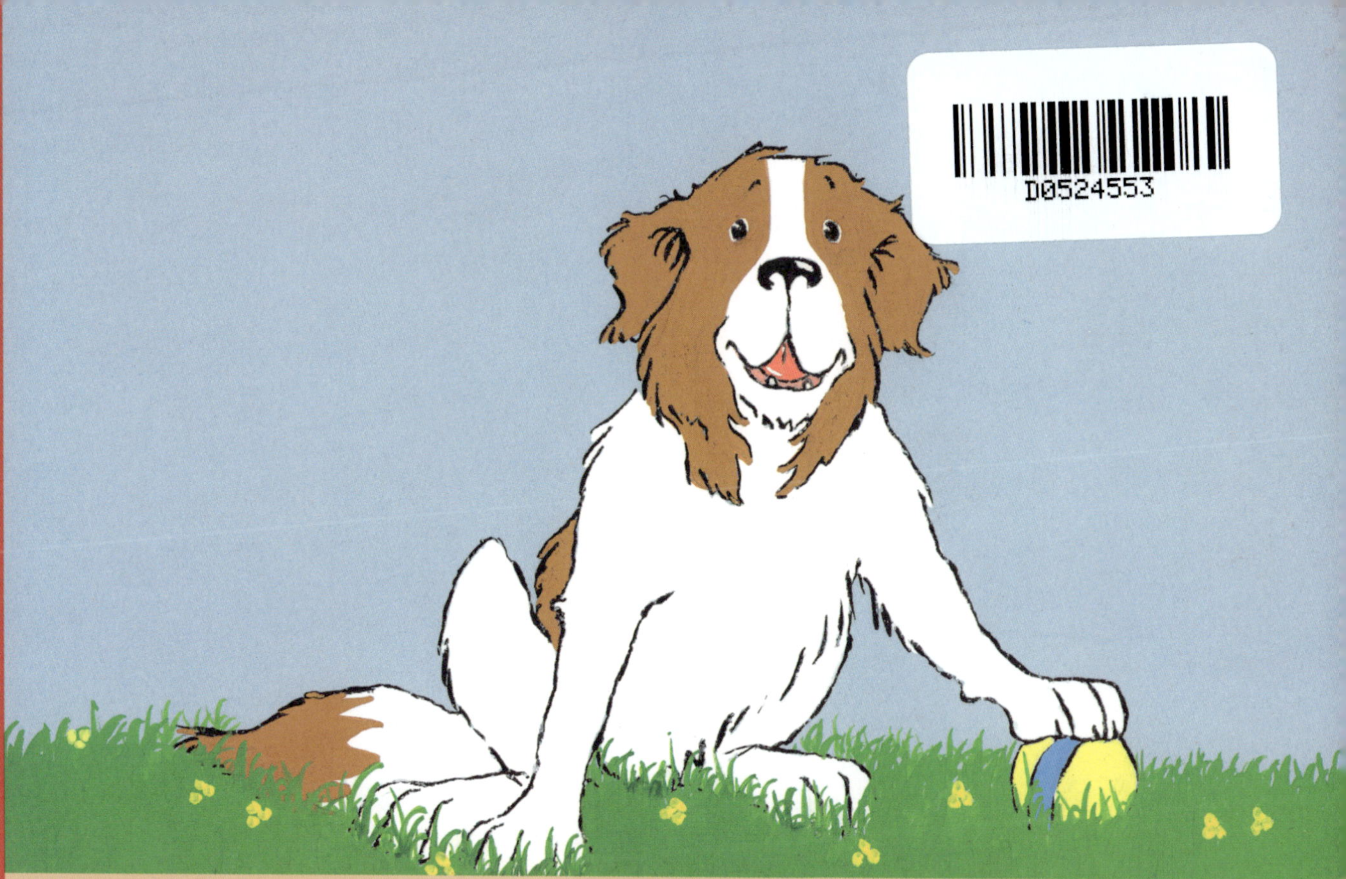

This is Winnie's ball.

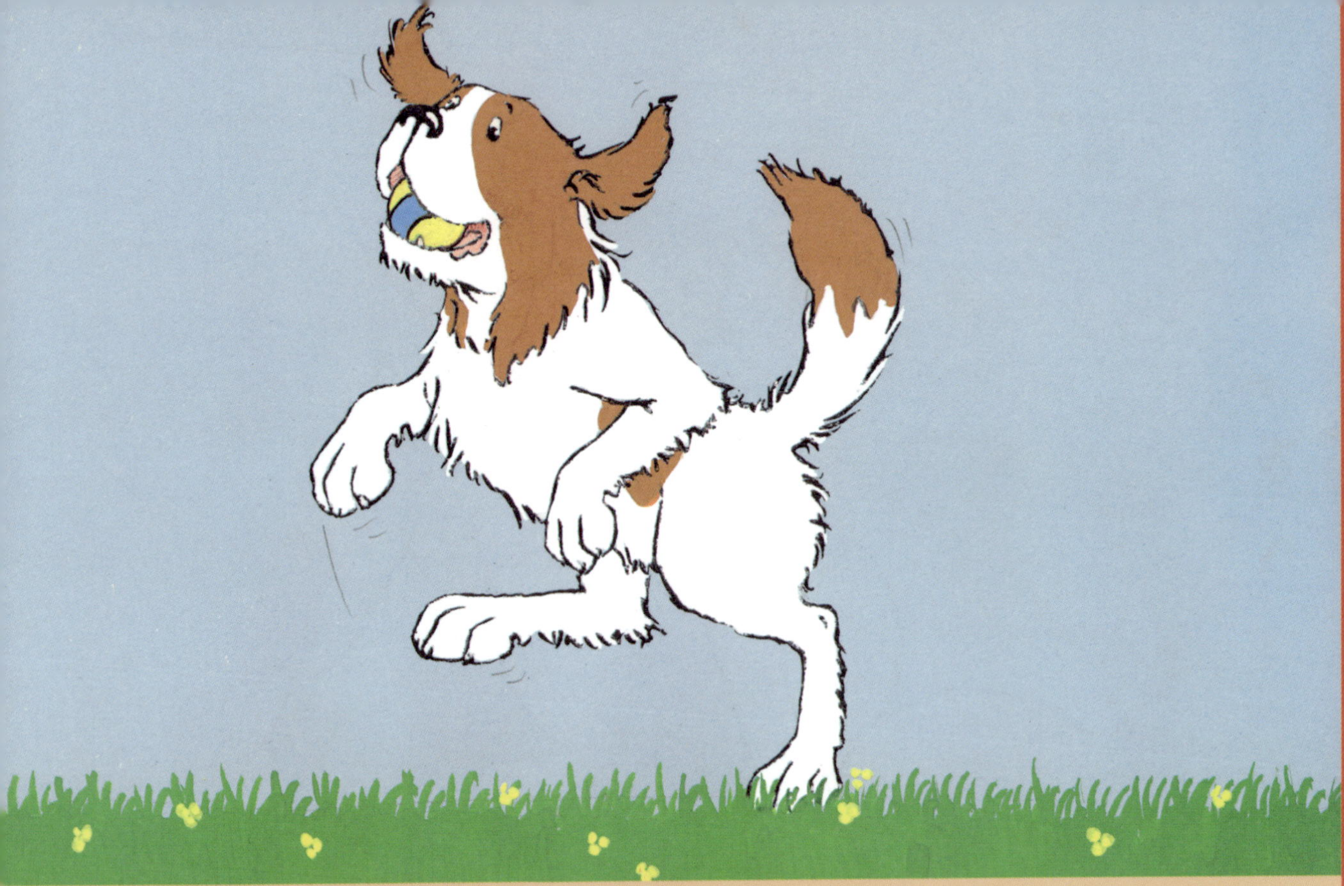

Winnie catches her ball.

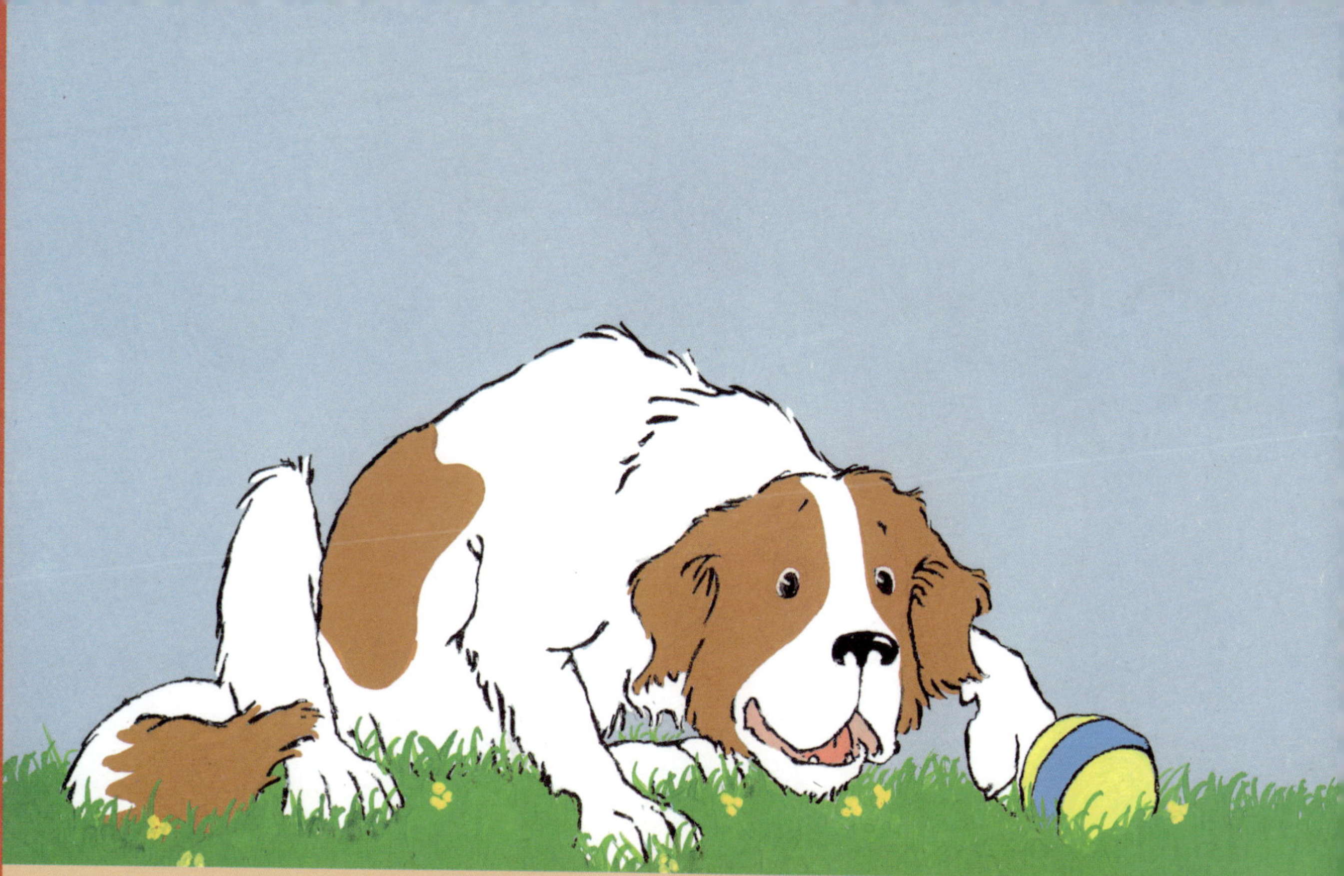

Winnie rolls her ball.

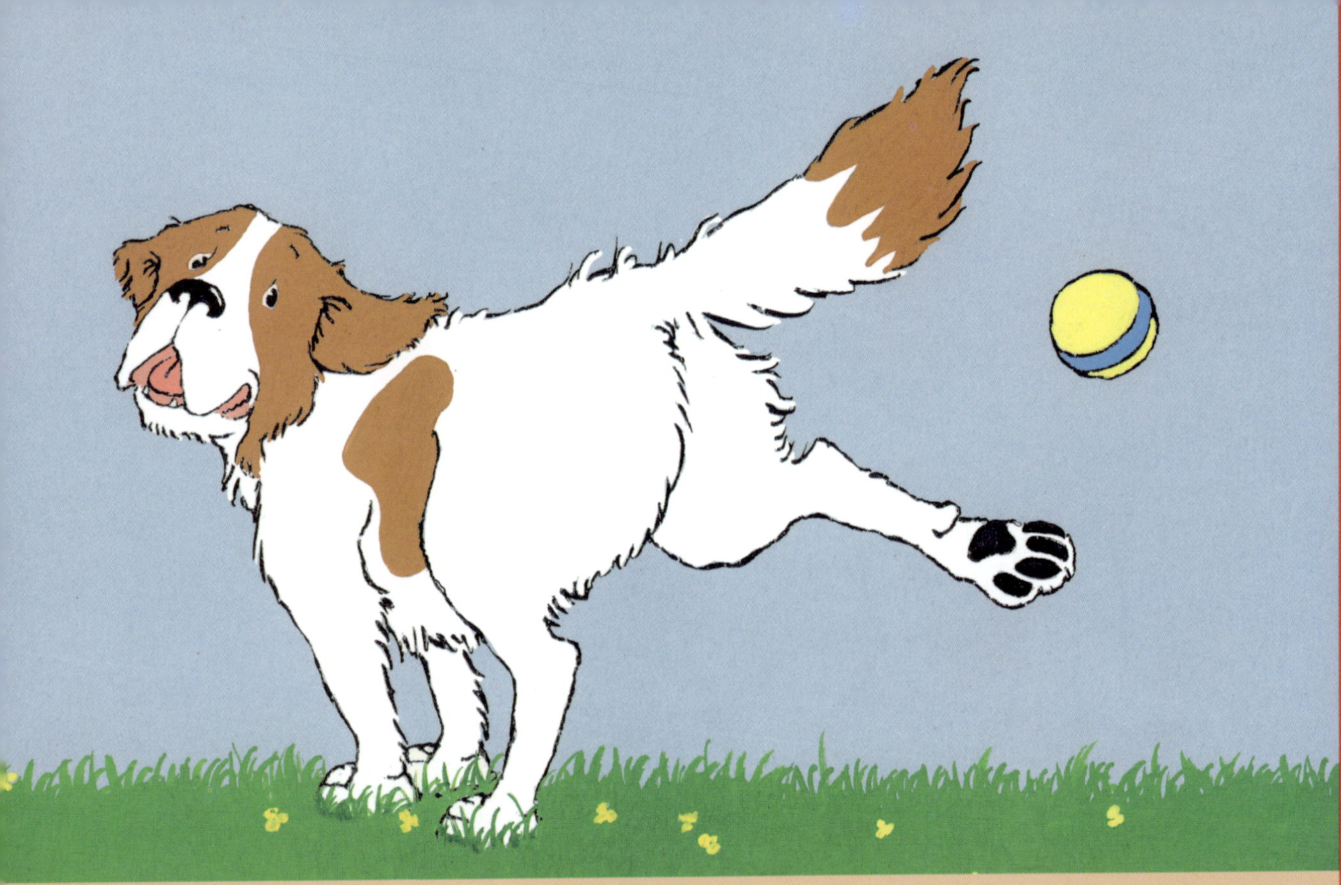

Winnie kicks her ball.

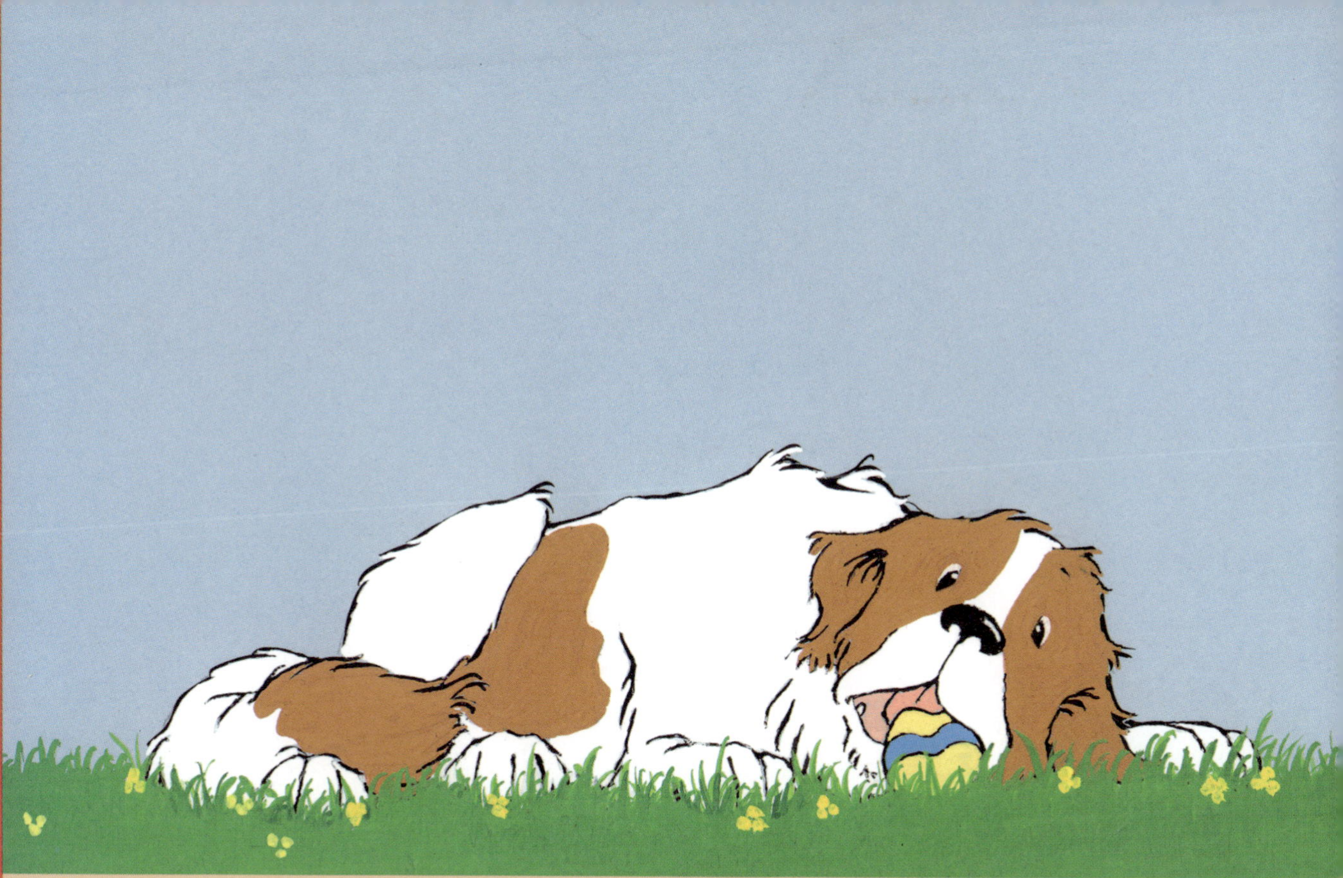

Winnie chews her ball.

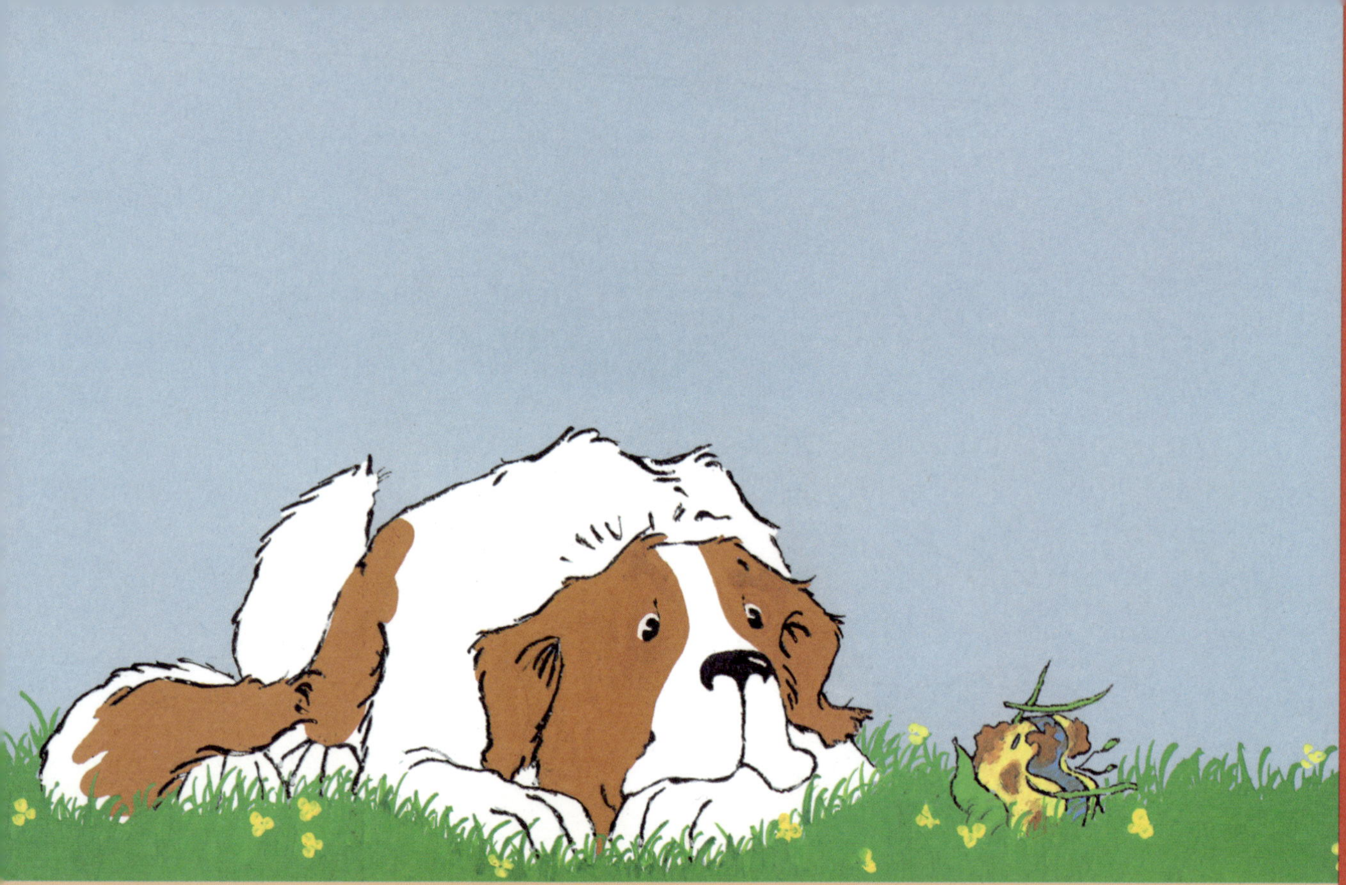

Winnie's ball is yucky.

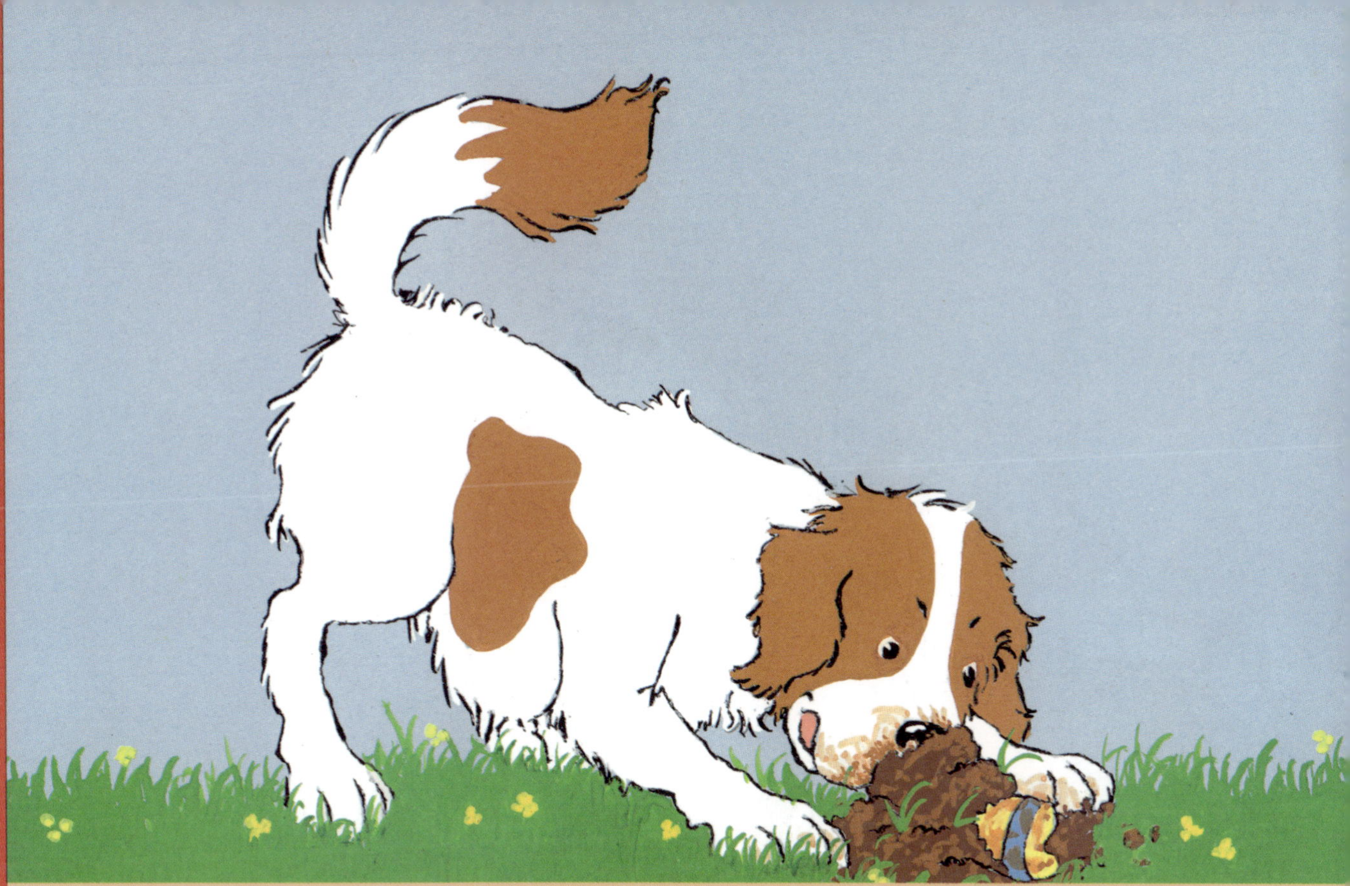

Winnie buries her ball.

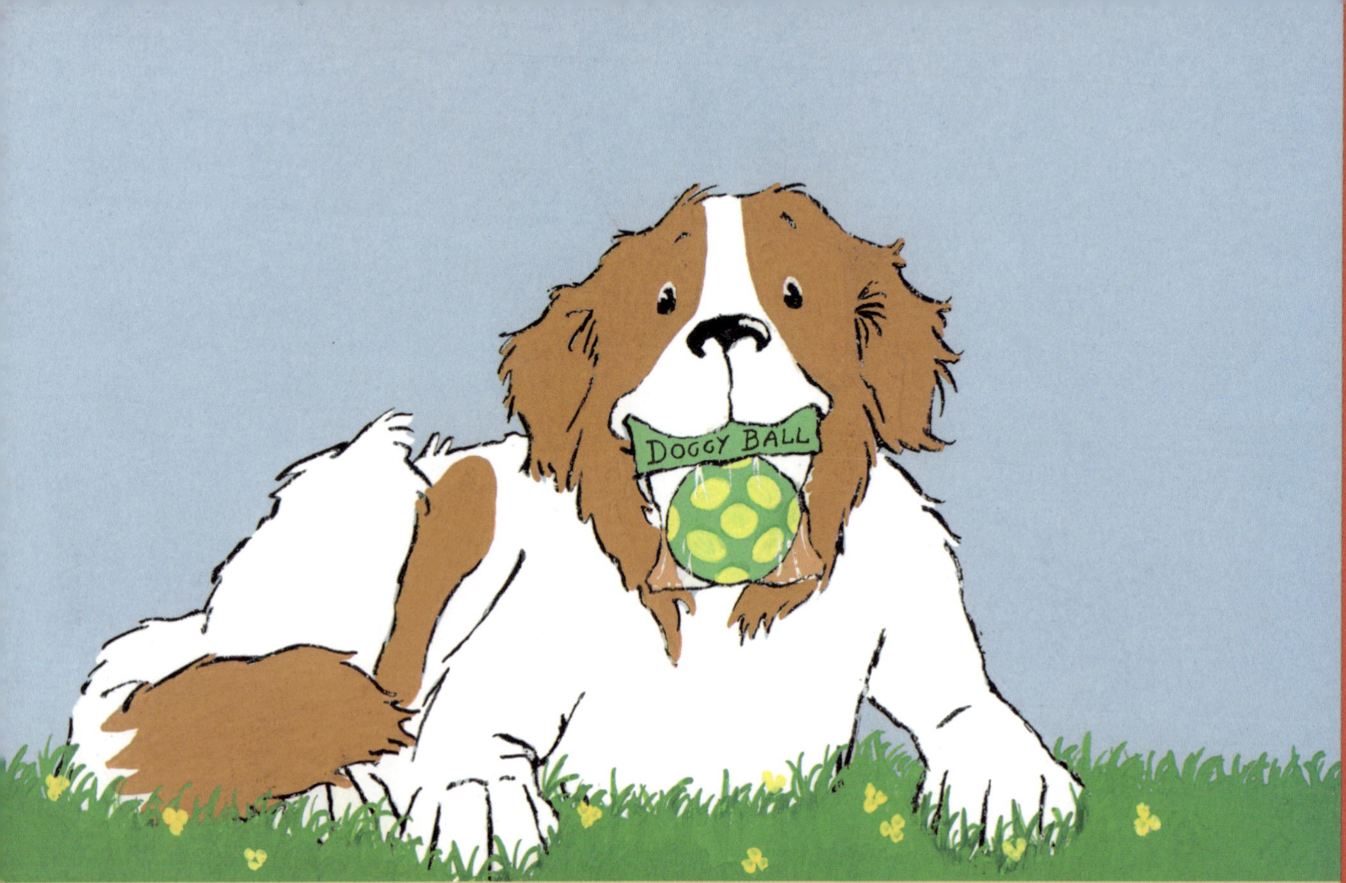

This is Winnie's NEW ball.